This book belongs to

....

....

PUFFIN BOOKS

UK | USA | Canada | Ireland | Australia | India | New Zealand | South Africa

Puffin Books is part of the Penguin Random House group of companies whose
addresses can be found at global.penguinrandomhouse.com

First published by Ladybird Books 2004
This edition published by Puffin Books 2017
001

Manufactured in China

A CIP catalogue record for this book is available from the British Library

ISBN: 978–0–241–32648–0

All correspondence to:
Puffin Books, Penguin Random House Children's
80 Strand, London, WC2R 0RL

Spot's
New Game

Eric Hill

Spot and Tom were in the garden.
"When you've finished on the
swing, can we play a game?"
asked Tom.
"OK," said Spot. "Let's play
hide-and-seek."
"That's not much fun with just
the two of us," said Tom.

Just then, Helen and Steve looked over the fence.

"Yoo-hoo, Spot!" said Helen.
"Can we play with you and Tom?"
"Yes!" said Spot. "We can play
hide-and-seek. You can hide and
I'll shut my eyes and count
to ten. Then watch out!"

9

Spot started to count. Helen, Tom and Steve ran around finding places to hide.

"One, two, three…" said Spot.

"Where shall I hide?" said Helen.

Tom and Steve had disappeared
and Spot was still counting.
"Four, five, six…" said Spot.

Then, Helen found a hiding place.

"Seven, eight, nine...ten!" Spot opened his eyes. "Here I come!"

Spot looked around. There was no sign of Helen, or Tom, or Steve.

16

Spot looked behind the fence.
"Nobody there," said the
blue bird, as it flew away.

Spot walked past a rose bush.
"Mmm, that's a nice smell,"
said Spot.

Then Spot stopped. He heard a
noise coming from behind the bush.
It was a giggle – definitely
a giggle!

"I've never heard a bush giggle,"
said Spot, and he looked behind
the bush.

"Found you, Helen!" said Spot.
"I heard you giggle."
"Oops!" said Helen. "I was
enjoying myself too much!"

19

Spot carried on looking for
the others, but there was no sign
of Tom or Steve. Spot even looked
inside the wheelbarrow.

"You woke me up!" said Ginger
cat. "I was having a nice dream."
"Sorry!" said Spot.

21

Spot went a bit further
down the garden path and
stopped by a tree. He heard
another giggle.

"I haven't heard a tree giggle,
either," said Spot.

He looked up and shouted,
"Come down, Steve! I heard
you giggle."

Steve jumped down from
the tree.
"Have you found Tom yet?"
he asked.
"Not yet," said Spot.

Suddenly, a loud noise came
from the shed and a rabbit
jumped out from behind a
flowerpot. Then Spot heard
another giggle.

Spot opened the shed door and
there was Tom.

"What was that noise?"
asked Spot.
"Oh, I was giggling so much
I knocked down a flowerpot,"
said Tom. "I like this game...
if only I could stop giggling!"

"Well," said Spot, "now that
I've found everyone, I think
we should play the game again.
That was fun."

Helen smiled.
"Yes, but this time we can call the
game hide-and-giggle!"

And that started off another round of giggles.